The Rabbit on the Moon

Moon photo courtesy of: Artur Ziętala

For
Scott & Penny

Phoebe is a rabbit
who loves to jump about.

See Phoebe with her friends,
as they play and laugh and shout.

"I'm the greatest jumper," called Phoebe to them all.

Then with a hop, skip and a jump, she leapt over a wall!

"How high can you jump?" they asked,
"Can you jump over a car?"

Well imagine their surprise
that a rabbit could jump so far!

Bee looked on in wonder,
as Phoebe yelled, "Watch me!"

Then with a mighty leap,
she jumped over a tree!

"How about that?" said Phoebe.
"Not high enough," said mouse.

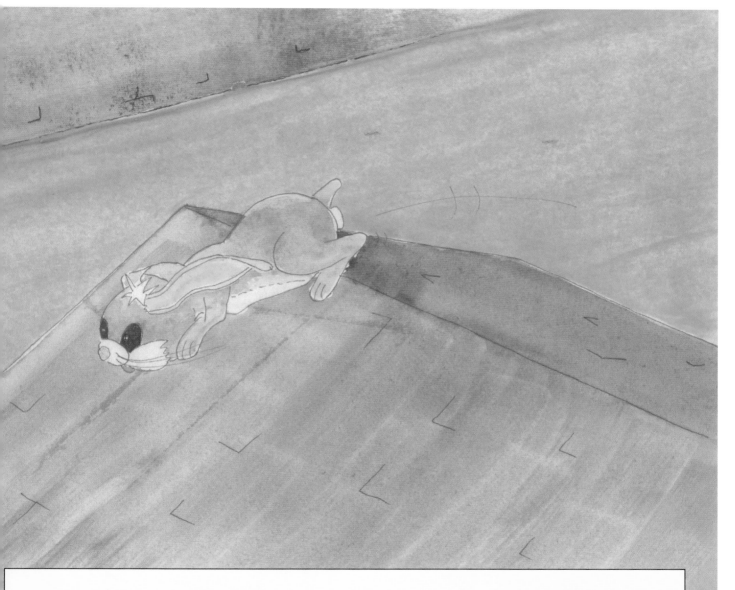

So Phoebe gathered all her strength and jumped over a house!

But the cow was not impressed and as she hummed a merry tune...

...she took a long run up
and jumped right over the moon!

"That's easy," said Phoebe
"The moon is not so high."

So she took a running jump
and leapt into the sky.

Up and up and up she went
so high into the night.

All her friends watched wide-eyed,
it was such a thrilling sight.

Phoebe tried to match the cow
and be a copycat...

...but didn't jump quite high enough and landed with a 'SPLAT!'

So all you boys and girls
when bedtime comes so soon,
look up and wave 'night night'
to the Rabbit on the Moon.

So now you've read the story,
when the moon is full and bright.
Look up and see the rabbit
and wave with all your might!

Printed in Great Britain
by Amazon